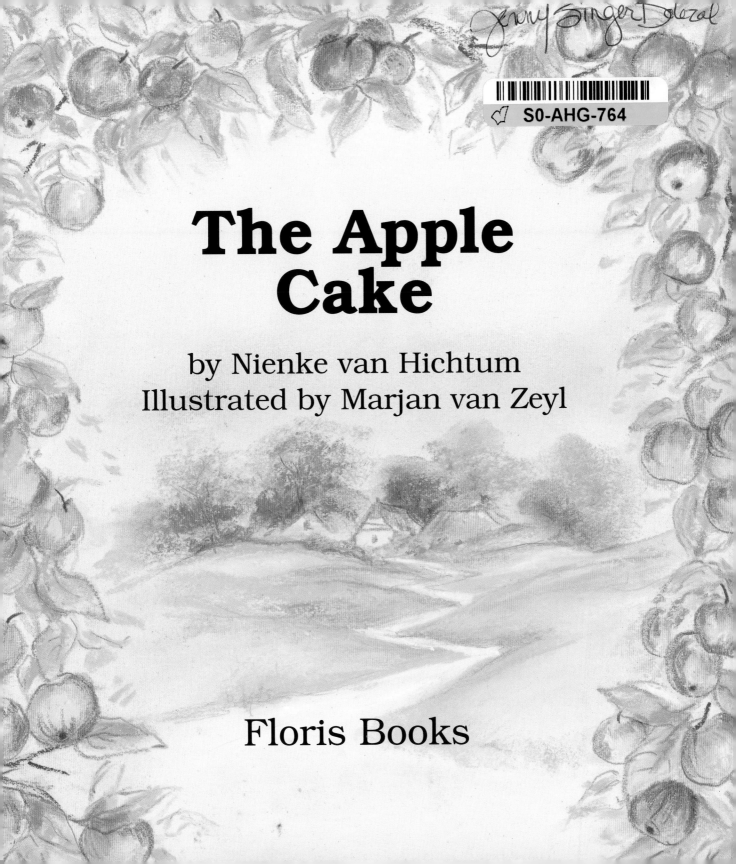

The Apple Cake

by Nienke van Hichtum
Illustrated by Marjan van Zeyl

Floris Books

There was an old woman who took a fancy one day to eat an apple cake. She had plenty of flour, sugar and butter, and enough spices. But the one thing she had not got was an apple. She did have plums: a whole tree full of plums, the roundest and reddest that you ever saw. Well, you just cannot make an apple cake from plums, even if you try your very hardest!

The more the old woman thought about it, the more she wanted an apple cake and nothing else would do. So she set off to market to look for apples. But first she took a basket, filled it with plums and covered them with a snow-white napkin.

"Well," she thought, "it may happen that I come to a place where there *are* apples but no plums."

She had not gone very far before she came to a field where hens, geese and turkeys were running about. What a hubbub and a cackling! And in the middle of them stood a young woman scattering grain. The young woman nodded to the old woman in a friendly way and before long the two of them were chatting away happily together. The young woman told the old woman all about her hens, geese and turkeys, and the old woman told the young woman how much she wanted an apple cake but she only had a basket of plums with her in the hope that she could exchange them for some apples.

"Well, well," exclaimed the young woman, "isn't that a lovely basket of plums! Let me tell you, my husband loves nothing better than plum-jelly. But I have no apples to swop with you. The only thing I could give you is a bagful of feathers, but that's hardly enough, is it?"

"Ah, well, what I say is this," said the old woman, "better one person happy than two disappointed. Just hold out your apron."

And right away she emptied her basket of plums into the young woman's apron. In exchange she was given a bagful of feathers and she trotted off even more cheerily than before, saying to herself: "Although I am no nearer to my apple cake, at least I'm no further, and one thing is certain: feathers are lighter than plums."

Up the hill she went, and down again. Then she came to a garden full of beautiful lilies, lilac, violets, roses, every kind of blossom. Never had she seen such a lovely garden! She stopped to look at the flowers, and there she saw a man and a woman sitting in the garden, and heard them quarrelling.

"Wadding!" said the woman.

"No! straw!" said the man.

"No, indeed."

"Yes indeed."

There they were screaming at each other until they noticed the old woman standing by the gate. Then the wife said to her husband:

"Wait, *she* will say which of us is right."

So they beckoned to the old woman to come into the garden, and the wife said:

"Tell us, my dear, what you would use to stuff the cushion for your grandfather's chair. You'd use wadding, wouldn't you?"

"No, of course not," said the old woman.

"See, I told you," said the man, "straw is much better and it's fine and handy to get from the barn."

But the old woman shook her head.

"Oh no," she said, "I would never fill a cushion with straw."

It would be hard to say which of the two was the more disappointed. But the old woman showed them her bag of feathers.

"Look," she said, "a cushion stuffed with feathers is fit for a king. If you wish, I'll give you this bag of feathers for some apples or some flowers from your garden."

The man and the woman were very sorry that they had no apples but they had plenty of flowers, and you can imagine how glad they were to get the precious feathers for a handful of flowers.

"Ah, ha," exclaimed the woman, "there's nothing better than feathers to fill a cushion!"

And the man said: "My mother had a feather-cushion."

They laughed and smiled like happy children, and then they went round the garden gathering the loveliest flowers for the old woman: roses, lilies, lilac, violets — what a beautiful bouquet!

"That was a good swop," said the old woman. She was so glad she had helped to end the quarrel, and with a happy face she laid the flowers carefully in her basket. The man and the woman wished her well and off she went on her way.

A little further on she saw a handsome young man coming towards her. He was dressed in his very best clothes for he was going to visit his sweetheart. He would have been even more handsome had his face not looked so gloomy, as if he had not a friend in the whole wide world.

"It's a nice day, sir," said the old woman.

"Nice or nasty, fine or foul, good or bad," said the young man, "I don't care. My jeweller has not finished the ring that I ordered for my sweetheart. Now I'm going to her empty-handed."

"Better to go with empty hands than with an empty heart," said the old woman. "But we're only young once, and so I'll give you something to fill your empty hands, even though I won't get my apple cake."

So saying she took the flowers from her basket and gave them to the young man. At once his face lit up, the frown vanished from his forehead, and now he was the handsomest and finest young man that ever the sun shone down upon.

"Fair exchange is no robbery," said he, laughing, and taking a gold chain from his neck he dropped it into the old woman's basket. Then off he strode, carrying the flowers joyfully.

The old woman was quite overcome with her good fortune.

"For this gold chain I can buy up the whole apple-stall, and still have a tidy sum left over," said she to herself and trotted along even more briskly towards the market.

But she had hardly gone ten yards before she saw a poor woman with her two children sitting on the doorstep of a tumbledown cottage, all of them looking as miserable as she herself was happy. She stopped to ask kindly:

"Why are you looking so sad, my dear?"

"Why indeed," said the poor woman, "when you've eaten your last crust and there isn't a penny in the house to buy more."

"Well," said the old woman, "never let it be said that I enjoyed a nice apple cake while my neighbour went hungry."

With that she let the gold chain fall into the poor woman's lap and off she went without waiting for thanks. But she had not gone far before the poor woman came running after her.

"I haven't got much, dear lady, but here is a little dog for you, a nice friendly little creature to keep you company when you are alone. And may God bless you."

The old woman could not refuse and so she put the little dog into her basket and he seemed to like that very much.

"A bag of feathers for a basketful of plums, a bouquet of flowers for a bag of feathers, a gold chain for a bouquet of flowers, a little dog and a blessing for a gold chain — all giving and receiving, giving and receiving, and who knows, I may yet come home with some apples." That was what the old woman said to herself as she trotted along.

And see — she had not walked for five minutes before she saw in a garden an apple-tree laden with lovely red apples. On a bench in front of the house was sitting an old man.

"What a lovely apple-tree!" called out the old woman when she saw him.

"Yes, yes," said the old man, "but red apples are poor company when you are lonely. I would not miss them if I had a cheery little dog barking on my doorstep."

"Woof, woof, bow, wow!" said the little dog in the old woman's
basket, and one moment later there stood the dog barking happily
on the old man's doorstep. And the old woman was on her way
home with her basket full of lovely red apples.